In the Days of
Sand and
Stars

In the Days of Sand and Stars

MARLEE PINSKER

Illustrated by FRANÇOIS THISDALE

Tundra Books

Published in Canada by Tundra Books,
75 Sherbourne Street, Toronto, Ontario M5A 2P9

Published in the United States by Tundra Books of Northern New York,
P.O. Box 1030, Plattsburgh, New York 12901

Library of Congress Control Number: 2005910620

Library and Archives Canada Cataloguing in Publication

Pinsker, Marlee
    In the days of sand and stars / Marlee Pinsker ; François Thisdale (illustrator).

ISBN 13: 978-0-88776-724-1
ISBN 10: 0-88776-724-9

    1. Legends, Jewish – Juvenile literature.   2. Midrash – Juvenile literature.
3. Women in the Bible – Juvenile literature. I. Thisdale, François, 1964- II. Title.

BM530.P55 2006   j296.1'420521   C2005-907304-7

ONTARIO ARTS COUNCIL
CONSEIL DES ARTS DE L'ONTARIO

We acknowledge the financial support of the Government of Canada through the
Book Publishing Industry Development Program (BPIDP) and that of the Government
of Ontario through the Ontario Media Development Corporation's Ontario Book
Initiative. We further acknowledge the support of the Canada Council for the Arts and
the Ontario Arts Council for our publishing program.

The illustrations for this book were digitally rendered

Printed and bound in China

1 2 3 4 5 6   11 10 09 08 07 06

For my father, Morris, and my mother, Edith,

who first taught me to look for

the stories behind the stories.

– M.P.

To Nini,

through whose eyes I see.

– F.T.

Contents

Foreword

These stories are written in the tradition of *midrash*, which means they explore the Biblical text to find new insights for our times. We weave stories into the areas in which the text is silent, giving voices to the people we want to understand. In this way, we imagine ourselves into the words of the Bible and bring its meanings forward, into our own lives. As I wrote these stories, I heard Sarah's laughter and considered Eve's questions. I was sad for Dina, but I rejoiced in the promise of Yocheved's life.

The Bible is a great gift, and its meanings are gradually revealed to us as we wrestle with our own lives. I hope the connection with these women enriches your life as much as it has enhanced mine.

The First Woman, Eve

The first animals were like all those that followed. They weren't surprised by much, because they took things for granted the way animals do. But the woman made them stop chewing their vegetables and look up.

First of all, she could speak their language. Adam had named them, but the woman could speak to them. Adam stood upright, but the woman was always bending down to hear what the mice had to say, climbing up to hear what the tree sloths were humming about. The woman could speak, and she used her speech to ask questions.

She realized that the earth had been there longest. In those days the earth could speak in words, so she asked for the whole history. She was interested in hearing about the horrible confusion of the disorder of chaos, when great gobs of everything were whirling about: mud, water, lightning, rocks, salt, brimstone, fire, and silt, all flying through the air. She wanted to hear about the first light,

before the sun and the moon were created, and she was interested in the water that was separated and moved above the heavens so the land could appear. The land had liked this. It felt good that part of it was dry and part wet, and told her how gentle the rain was on its grasses.

The woman stroked the earth, which could be heard to purr up against her like a cat. She stroked the grasses and found out that they had sprung up on the third day, along with all the rest of the vegetation. The woman was disappointed that she couldn't seem to communicate with the sun or the moon, but she dove into the water to find the fish. She learned about their quiet world beneath the sea. The leviathans, huge sea creatures, told her about the four rivers bounding Eden.

Bounding? The woman didn't know about this word, and for the first time thought about limitations. She found Adam naming the great cats, and interrupted him.

"Adam, did you know we have great boundaries around us? What do you think would be beyond the great rivers? Can we cross them if we want to?"

Adam told her to investigate Eden first. He had a job to do. A lion roared its approval of *Lion*, and Adam turned to the ocelot.

The woman found the snake and sat down beside the Tree of the Knowledge of Good and Evil. Its fruit smelled better than anything else in the garden, each one a different, beautiful, vibrant color.

"Take a bite," said her friend the snake.

"We are not supposed to," said the woman.

"That's not a reason," said the snake.

Now, the woman didn't know how to argue. She had no other arguments to make. She didn't know about bad faith or trickery, and she knew the snake had been around a lot longer than she had, so she plucked a piece of the fruit and looked at it.

"It is yummy," said the snake.

The woman smelled it and almost swooned.

"It is impossible to resist."

The woman couldn't resist. She took a bite.

"Thank you," she said to the snake. "It was good, and why would it be here if God didn't want us to eat it? I'll run and tell Adam."

The woman took the delicious fruit to Adam, and he asked of her even fewer questions than she had asked of the snake. What did he know? As soon as he ate, he looked at the woman and noticed they were naked. The two of them quickly got up to find some fig leaves with which to cover themselves.

For the first time they noticed the animals always went about their tasks of eating and sleeping and running and drinking without thought. For the first time, they weren't sure of what to do. They walked through Eden, hand in hand, watching the water and the land and the weeds and the birds and the fish and the insects and the animals.

They heard the sound of the Lord God moving in the Garden at the breezy time of day. Adam pulled his wife to hide among the trees. For a moment the woman held back, yearning to listen.

When the Lord God saw the man and the woman and noticed they were hiding, the Lord God inquired of them. The man said he hid because he was embarrassed. He said the woman had given him the fruit to eat. God said to the woman, "What is this that you have done?"

The woman had never spoken to God before. She had spoken to the earth, the fish, the waters, the animals — and here was God, even more impressive in some indefinable way than all the rest. This Voice promised compassion and wisdom and guidance and an insight bigger than she could imagine. It made her think of a Tree of Life, with its roots in Eden and its crown reaching up to the heavens without boundary; limitless, soaring, beyond all thought.

First, she answered truthfully, sharing the credit, "The serpent tricked me. (Ah! So this is what it was!) Then, being the woman that she was, she asked where God had gotten the idea to have such a magnificent world. She had no idea what the pangs of childbirth could be, but she was willing to try it. She asked when she could have a name of her own. She wanted a name. She asked if they would really get a chance to go beyond the boundaries of Eden. Newly imbued with the concepts of good and evil, she asked whether there had to be good to have evil, and whether there had to be evil in order to have good. God stepped back, Adam stepped forward. Adam said, "Well, she needs a name, doesn't she?

Adam and Eve were taken beyond the boundaries of the Garden of Eden and forbidden to return. Adam knew he had to work hard to make a living from the earth, and Eve (a name!) worked hard, and she also gave birth to several children. During this time she continued to think of questions, but as time passed, she asked fewer of them aloud as she had to work so hard she often became exhausted. Eventually she narrowed them down to two.

In the twilight of her life, she asked how God could have been more present in their lives as they faced the conflicts of living outside the peaceful Garden. When God did not answer she asked why her son Abel had to die.

We are still trying to answer these questions.

Naamah, Listening

Naamah watched the animals entering the Ark from the highest deck. She saw some slithering and some hopping, some lurching and some walking slowly, scared half to death by the strange sound of their hooves on planed wood. She heard the shouts from within as Noah and their three sons pushed the animal pairs into the cages they had constructed.

These animals had never been inside anything more confining than a forest. They moaned and roared as they were prodded into the cages. Three decks of cages would be put to sea as the waters increased. Naamah had happily supervised the gathering of foods and seeds to be kept on the Ark. Now, however, she watched sadly. The Ark would be the world's biggest prison.

Noah and their grown sons, Shem, Cham, and Yaphet, came to join her, satisfied with their labors. Naamah accepted their hugs and offered them dinner. She and her daughters-in-law had set up sleeping quarters for the family on the Ark, and the men fell,

exhausted, into bed. Her sons' wives cleaned up after dinner and went to join their husbands. Naamah took a walk into the pit of misery beneath. Not a single animal could sleep. The noise was deafening.

When she lingered on the first deck, Naamah saw some of their neighbors who had come to jeer at them.

"I see you, Naamah! Are you up there choosing the best steak for yourself?"

"Hey! Noah! Who knew you loved animals that much? You want to live with chickens!"

"Look at the Noah family! They know how crazy people think they are, so they've surrounded themselves with animals and birds. Wait until the cuckoos tell you what you really are."

Naamah looked up at the stars. Here on earth, the animals were miserable and the people were miserable. She had no idea if the fish in the sea below were happy. The stars shone, laughing over everything.

The morning that the Flood began was quiet. The sunrise was brief and misty. A dawning of thin, yellow light gradually waned as the clouds moved in. Naamah stood watching. Noah came to stand next to her, putting his arm around her shoulders. He was much taller than she was. Their neighbors had once remarked they looked like an ape and a chipmunk standing together. No, they argued with some passersby, Noah and Naamah looked like a bull and a goat. The people decided among themselves that any children of Noah and Naamah's would look like hyenas; horrible crossbreeds. They thought that was hilarious, but Noah and

Naamah had just looked at each other and shrugged. This was their community.

Naamah leaned her head back against her husband's chest. "This is the beginning."

Noah nodded, pointing below. "You can see that waters are gushing out of the earth already. Wave goodbye to our house, it is sinking below."

Soon everything was sinking below. And there was no time to wave goodbye.

Noah and his sons rushed around to the animals, pitching straw and distributing hay. The wives took on the task of feeding the birds in their cages. Everyone had to carry buckets of waste material to throw over the sides. Even as the Ark slowly rose while the water level deepened, the family was becoming exhausted.

Far away and long ago, it seemed, the calls of the drowning people had diminished. Naamah thought she would never forget the sounds of their neighbor's hatred:

"Why didn't you build a boat for us?"

"Why are you saving the animals and leaving the people who love you?"

"Naamah! You are beautiful! You and Noah are the loveliest couple the world has ever seen! Save us!"

"Noah, don't turn your back! You are a donkey, Noah, and your wife is a rat. May you be cursed forever. . . ."

Naamah listened to the sound of the rain for the first two weeks; rain that fell like stones from the sky, all day and all night. The first of the animals began to die off, and the family went without sleep as they tried to stave off the deaths. Creatures that would never be seen again on this earth closed their eyes in despair.

Naamah walked the Ark weeping. She saw sad gorillas, staring out through their bars. Giraffes couldn't straighten their necks, and lay still, curled up on straw. She picked up the little furred bodies of the wensil bears, the first to go. She wanted to bury them, she wanted them to be remembered. She trudged to the deck to throw off the still male first, and then the little sad body of the female. She went back inside and leaned on a cage and wept.

A voice in her ear mocked her, "You are weeping, yesss, because your mother didn't lissssten like Eve did."

Naamah looked up quickly. Her mother had been one of the people cursing them as the waters began flowing. Naamah had begged her parents to build a boat of their own for four years before the flood.

"Eve," the voice continued. "Didn't she know us all, the snakes like me, and the voices of all the animals...."

Naamah hated snakes. She pulled away from the enclosure it was trapped in. "Lissssten...." It said again.

Naamah ran to the depths of the Ark, deep into the hold where the hippos lay groaning. Then she began walking up, searching out each compartment in the boat, looking at each animal carefully, and listening for the sounds of its language. If she could understand a snake, she could understand a weasel, right? How about the whines of a fox? The humming of the llamas? The baas of the sheep? Naamah closed her eyes.

How had Eve done it?

Naamah fell asleep on a pile of hay on the second level. In the night she opened her eyes and saw Noah, her large, hardworking husband, leaning on the pitchfork, shaking with exhaustion. She called him over and told him to lie down with her. He collapsed beside her.

"We have to listen…" she said, but drifted into sleep again, dreaming of a dry dawn on a rocky hill.

Naamah was awakened by a soft voice near her head. "I'm itching all over and I need a good scratching post." She opened her eyes, laughing, and a cougar was stretching in a nearby cage. She thrust her hand right inside its prison and scratched its fur.

"Good, good," it said.

Naamah woke Noah and told him to listen. She reached her hand inside the cage to touch the cougar again, and Noah grabbed her shoulder and pulled her back.

"Are you crazy?" he said.

"Can't you hear it talking?"

"That's growling, Naamah, and it wants to eat your hand."

Naamah argued with Noah for two days; called her sons and their wives over and argued with them. No one agreed with her. Still, the deaths were mounting. And each death meant a species that would never live again.

Naamah woke up one night and began another walk around the Ark. This time she spoke as she walked, spoke in a humming, growling, sighing language that she made up. The snake stuck its forked tongue out approvingly. The birds twittered weakly from their small cages.

It was a simple message, really. There was enough food aboard for all, and they only had to refrain from eating each other. Naamah walked from cage to cage, asking for their agreement.

"Elephants, what say you?"

"Lions, what say you?"

"Giraffes, what say you?"

"Who is for freedom, within constraints?"

"Who dares to walk free on this small world?"

"Not the mongoose," argued the snake. "You can't trust them."

"NO!" Naamah said, and she was understood in every language. "We will all work. We will all help. We will all respect each other. We will create Eden once again. Here."

There was great debate in a thousand different throats. They finally came to an agreement.

"Freedom," each voice said.

"With responsibility!" insisted Naamah.

"Yes."

"Yes."

"Yes."

"Yesssss."

It rained for twenty-six more days. The boat floated for another one hundred and fifty days.

Inside the Ark, Naamah had freed the animals and each did its job, toting straw, distributing food, hauling out the waste in baskets on their backs. The horses gave the people rides from one end of the Ark to the other, and the birds sang happy songs to pass the day. The giraffes stretched their spotted necks and delicate, horned heads to the sky. The snakes slithered from one to another, sharing news and urging patience. Around the cages Naamah used some seeds she had collected to plant vines and flowers, so that the horrible little hellhole bloomed green and beautiful.

Even Naamah looked on with wonder, as plantings that should have taken whole seasons to grow and attain complexity and fullness, leafed out and greened up and sprouted flowers that bloomed overnight, to the delight of the hummingbirds and bees. Oaks rose and pushed through from one deck to another and shed acorns; the squirrels and monkeys gathered nuts and berries.

Noah put his arm around his tiny wife. He would never forget the day he had awoken and seen the order that she had created overnight on their small world. He watched in wonder as butterflies landed on her shoulders and deer stood conversing with her by the flicker of their eyelashes and the touch of their noses.

Noah never learned to talk with the animals as his wife could, but he learned to watch them and anticipate their needs. Somewhere, when the waters receded, he would once again build and plan. For now, he looked to Naamah, with her small body and giant understanding. Naamah, whose idea had been like a tiny seed that had taken root in a second, brief Garden of Eden.

3

Sarai: Something Wonderful

In Ur of the Chaldees, a young girl named Sarai picked up soft, white rags and made her way to the back of her family's stone house.

It was Sarai's job to dust. She took her woolen cloths and walked slowly through the house, rubbing the dirt of the days from bare dun stone and polished wood. Heat rose from the stone flooring and baked down from the ceiling. Sarai walked barefoot from one small room to another.

If she worked fast, she could finish before her brother came home and be sitting next to her mother, safe. She made her way from one room to another, finally turning to the alcove which held their household god. She folded the white cloth, preparing a clean surface.

Sarai climbed up on the altar and stood next to the statue, cleaning first the stony skull with its hard topknot, working her way down the smooth surface to the narrowed eyes and jutting

nose and grim mouth. When she heard voices in the hallway, she quickly climbed down and bowed three times before the god.

"Save me," she whispered. "I'll give you oil and barley." She was sure the statue nodded. She squeezed herself behind the god, and crouched in the shadows at its base.

The footsteps came closer. Sarai held her breath. She could smell Girot's presence, angry sweat under alcohol. The footsteps stopped. Sarai closed her eyes. It was all right. Maybe he was just looking at the figurine. But the rough laugh was not the way he addressed the god figure. It was the way he addressed her.

"Sarai's little dust cloth is in front of the god," he said, rolling each word like dry sand in his mouth. "A strange offering."

Sarai didn't move. But his breathing was coming closer.

The hard hand found her and hauled her out, bare feet scraping against the hard floor. His hand on her forearm was too tight.

"Show respect to the god!" He yelled at her as though she were across the marketplace. "Do you think he wants your dust cloth?" He held the little cloth crumpled in one fist and when she opened her mouth to gasp he shoved it in hard. Dry dust fuzz choked her, making her cough and flail.

His hand was squeezing so tight around her upper arm, he would be clutching bone any minute. Veins in his eyeballs stood out, fiery red, and his breath smelled like beer.

"You can't hide from me," he promised her, "I will always be able to find you. Your red hair is like a flag, telling me where you are."

Sarai pulled and struggled against him, fighting for breath.

He started laughing, "It's a chicken," the words were coming in short gasps, "It's trying to get away from the cookpot!"

Sarai twisted her arm up and back, pushing in the direction of his thumb, which gave way, finally, and she laughed to find herself free, and then ran as fast as she could toward the kitchen. Mother would be there. Away from Girot's rage and the god's unseeing eyes.

Mother stirred a pot, smiling at her story. "He's your brother, Sarai. You must show him respect. He didn't like the way you were treating our family god. Try to understand."

Sarai was still breathing hard, excited that she had gotten away from him. "He called me a chicken."

Mother laughed, "But not a hen, surely. You are more like a little rooster, crowing all day long."

Sarai clutched the white cloth, damp with her saliva and dirty with dust from the windowsills and the tables and the god with the blind eyes. She giggled, seeing herself as a rooster, crowing.

Avram was put in charge of his father's store. He walked up and down in front of the idols his father had carved, dusting their angry faces, putting dishes of food before them, watching their eyes and mouths for flashes of fiery feeling. He had been watching these idols for a long time. Although people gave them food and sometimes money, the idols they prayed to did not move or soften their stony stares.

A cat-headed god in front of the store looked out on the dusty street. It was a great favorite of the camel merchants who passed near the store. Avram had often seen them put mounds of seeds and nuts in the outstretched paws of the god. This was an interesting god for him, because lately, the food they placed in front of it seemed to disappear.

Avram sat in the shade of the store, watching.

He noticed when a small female figure walked toward the store. Well wrapped and veiled, she reached up to the plate of food in front of the god and brushed what was there into a clay bowl.

Avram pounced, grabbed the figure, spilled the food, and was totally unprepared for the scream of fury. "Look what you did! Now it's wasted for anyone!"

Avram took a step backwards, but held on tight to the owner of the voice. He held an arm, and started unwrapping from the head. As he pulled the cloth off, he recognized the young girl. "Sarai! What are you doing here?"

"What are *you* doing here? No one watches this old idol! He's been standing out here forever without being sold! Why aren't you watching the idols in the store?"

Avram said, "They aren't moving. But what would you do with this food? You're not hungry!"

Sarai wiggled out of his grasp easily, with a grace that came from long practice. She took the length of cloth in her hands and wrapped it around herself. Once again, the seventeen year old became an ageless, faceless female.

"There's a blind woman begging on this street," she said in a muffled voice. "Why doesn't this god of the street help her? Maybe the god needs me to walk down there with it."

Avram made a quick grab for her, and Sarai, laughing now, danced just beyond his grasp.

"I'll give you some food, Sarai. You can take it to the blind woman."

Avram brought some dates and nuts on a plate. He handed it to Sarai, who took it with a skinny little hand and a fast skip away.

"Wait!" Avram said as she turned.

The giggle came floating back down the street to him. She didn't wait.

Avram didn't wait either. He didn't know whether it was because of what she had done, or because of that silly laugh that shook his thoughts. For some reason it made him do something he had been thinking of. It took him all afternoon, and by the time his father came back home in the evening, he had smashed every idol in the store.

When the women gathered at the well that evening, they talked about how Avram had said that the idols had smashed each other. Someone had heard that he had been taken to Nimrod for judgment — and punishment. Everyone was angry at the boy who had dared to mock the gods. They didn't think it would go well with him.

"They'll burn him," one of the elderly women said.

"They won't bother," said another. "He'll be exiled to the caves beyond Nimrod's house, where there isn't enough food or water to keep a mouse alive."

"And he should be," the women agreed, dipping their pitchers for water. Above the splash and the gurgle, their voices blended in

agreement with each other. "Of course he should be," a woman with a baby in a sling against her body said. "He destroyed his father's work. He destroyed our only gods."

Sarai giggled under her breath. "And such delicate gods they are . . . ," which made the others stop talking for a minute. They stared at the thin figure that had let its scarf fall back to reveal a grinning face and bright hair that seemed to reflect the rosy skies of the setting sun. Then they started talking again, as though they had never seen her at all.

Sarai, listened at the well for a long time that evening. After the other women left with their pitchers, she filled her own and headed for Nimrod's. She didn't know why Avram had smashed the little gods, but she was sure it was a move in the right direction.

Sarah at the Well

here were ten women whispering by the well when Sarah came to fetch water. She could hear the play of their voices like water gurgling over the cool rocks. When they saw her they reached up eager hands to help her down the few steps to the mouth of the water, rimmed with stone.

"Let us help, Sarah. You are over ninety years old, you shouldn't still be carrying water."

"Never mind that she's over ninety and she shouldn't be carrying a baby."

"She's pregnant? How? At her age?"

"Shhh, children, let me sit," the old woman said. The cloth covering her head fell back, and white hair, like wispy cirrus clouds, framed her wrinkled face. She was the picture of old age, but her eyes were as alert and clear as a five year old's.

"And why shouldn't I be pregnant?" she asked. "My husband and I were promised a large family. It is time."

The women looked at each other, and, one by one, most of them got up to leave. "It's past time," one muttered as she went. "What kind of god lets a woman her age become . . ."

"I heard that," Sarah called out. "I'll tell you."

Six women sat down again by the well. They turned to Sarah and she smiled at them. "At one point in my life they said I was beautiful," she said. "I was so beautiful that kings wanted me. But look at me now. I am finally going to give birth, and all I've got left is my crow."

"Your what!?"

Sarah laughed. "My mother used to say I was like a rooster. I'm finally proving her wrong."

"At ninety?" said Hannah. "It's not natural."

Sarah said, "This will tell you God can do anything."

"People don't give birth at such an age," said Yavanna.

Sarah leaned forward, and her reflection in the pool got brighter. The setting sun lit the waters around her mirrored face and smoothed out the wrinkles of age, so that she looked down and recognized herself as she had looked years ago.

"My husband and I came on a long journey to this land. Our God changed our names to Sarah and Abraham and made us a promise: someday our descendants would be as many as the stars in the sky and the sands on the shores."

The women whispered to each other how unlikely that would be, coming from a childless old woman with white hair.

Sarah looked up at them, her brown eyes snapping, "Count the sands at your feet. Count them!"

"We can't!"

"And the stars?"

"We can't!"

Sarah's laugh was more like a rooster's crow this time.

One by one they left, shaking their heads. Only Tira stayed behind, dipping her pitcher into the cool waters, and then taking Sarah's pitcher and dipping it in for her.

"No good will come of this," said Tira.

"Oh, yes, great good will come of it," said Sarah. "But I won't be here to see it. My son will suffer and my people will suffer. I know already what lies in store for us."

"Then you must be sorry for the strangeness of this pregnancy."

Sarah shook her head. "When my children are confused by life, when they find it is strange and delivers its rewards like curses, I hope they will be able to laugh."

"You laughed when you found out?"

"Even God remarked on it. It is my gift to my people."

Tira picked up Sarah's pitcher and her own, helping Sarah settle hers on her head, as was customary. She watched as Sarah steadied it with one hand and walked off, swinging her hips. The old woman laughed as she walked, and people looked up at her in wonder.

She was giving birth at ninety, and she was hooting about it. The pregnancy was miracle enough, but combined with an elder's hoarse laughter, it was a wonder that would be remembered as long as Sarah's people met to talk and study.

And the truth is, she felt they would meet to talk and study and laugh like she did, for a long, long time.

5

Rebecca Comes Home

Rebecca left her house at sunset, the pitcher balanced carefully on her head. She took a deep breath as she walked outside, happy to be away from the household. Betuel, her father, and Laban, her brother, were still enjoying their afternoon nap, but her father's and brother's wives were already up and working and arguing, screaming and scheming. Her father and brother each had two wives, and they were attempting to make a common dinner, each in her own way, without consultation. A lamb was ready to be cooked, but the cooks seemed to be hacking at each other, rather than the meat. Pots were clanging, favorite knives were waved, and people were already weeping at the many injustices.

While everyone in the household snored and quarreled, wept and complained, only Deborah, Rebecca's old childhood nurse, worked in silence. As Rebecca passed through the courtyard, Deborah came toward her with a basket of olives in her arms. Deborah nodded to Rebecca and Rebecca nodded back.

Rebecca strode to the well, putting as much energy into her steps away from the house as possible. Could her brother really have told both of his wives that he wanted them to learn to sing like Esra, who lived nearby? The household was already a spider's web of accusation and bitterness. Now the smell of burning meat filled the air, and sour snatches of song from strained vocal cords rang out from each corner of the compound.

Every step she took away was like a blessing. The air seemed sweet and clean. The well was a rock mound built up around a hole, an inviting channel reaching into the depths of the earth. Rebecca saw graceful women there. All the younger daughters and lesser wives of the households came to the well, forced to do the hard work of dipping for the water, filling the jugs, and carrying the heavy burden back.

To her, the job was a delight. It took her away from her fractious household and gave her a chance to talk with her friends. Sometimes a stranger passed through, and she had a chance to learn something of the world outside Aram-Naharayim. She helped water the shepherds' sheep and the travelers' camels, and indeed, she would have been happy to stand there all day, dipping and carrying and listening.

Laila, who had played with her since they were babies, had come down to the well, and they met up together. Laila made Rebecca laugh, saying that she had already heard what was going on in Rebecca's house. Everyone had heard! Such weeping! Such singing! Laila affected an imitation of someone weeping and singing at the same time, sounding exactly like Rebecca's family in the house she had just left. Rebecca grinned, saying that only the smell of charring meat and the thunderous snores of men, still napping, while their women started the evening meal, were missing from Laila's performance.

It was Laila who first saw the dusty man, heading their way with ten camels. "I have to get home or my father will make *me* do the work of a camel," she whispered. "You should get your water fast so we can both leave together."

Rebecca agreed, helping Laila lower the rope deep into the earth and haul up the first bucket of water. She steadied Laila's pitcher while Laila poured the cold water in. The man with the camels looked tired. He was coming closer. He must have journeyed a long way, since the camels' humps were thin and crooked.

The man stroked his lead camel's long face. "I have to find him a wife," he muttered.

Laila whispered to Rebecca, "He's looking for a wife for his camel . . ." and Rebecca laughed.

"Oh, no," she warned Laila, giggling. "Run home fast, or you'll be leaving with him, with a saddle on your back. I'm not in such a hurry. I brought plenty of water back this morning. You know there are already too many women in my house. No one will care if I am a little late."

Laila touched her shoulder, waved a grateful goodbye, and was gone. Rebecca lowered the bucket into the earth as the stranger came to the well. Near her the other women pulled their veils around their faces. She raised her bucket as he talked and lifted it for him to drink from. He was grateful. He had just asked if anyone would give him a drink, and all the women had turned away from him.

Rebecca looked into his face while he drank, seeing a man with sunburned skin and a steady hand. She let him drink from her pitcher, while she hauled up more water for his camels. No one else offered to help. She did it herself, until her arms ached. Let no one say that the people of Aram Naharayim were inhospitable.

She hurried to pour water for all his camels while the women around her complained that they couldn't get enough water between her trips to the trough. It was taking too long. Rebecca smiled, rushing to get all the water into the trough before she got pushed out of the line altogether.

If Laila were here Rebecca would again offer her opinion that some people were too noisy in themselves, like the people in her family. Her father, Betuel, would stand outside and scream at his shepherds, and then come inside and scream at his wives with the same voice. Her brother, Laban, would whisper, causing all the people he passed to frown and scowl. He was a farmer planting seeds of unhappiness in long rows.

Laila's family was different. There was laughter among the women. Laila's father brought home new dyes for his wives to share. There was no crying behind a veil, scurrying figures bent over in sorrow when you turned a corner.

Rebecca finished watering the camels. The man kept looking at her, mumbling his thanks. At first she answered him. Then she realized that he was not thanking her, but speaking to someone she could not see – the God of Abraham – giving thanks for this wonderful girl who would, perhaps, be the person he was seeking. This invisible God was not entirely unknown to her. She watched, curious if the follower of this God would rise up angry and bitter, but was happy to see that he gave thanks and rose refreshed.

He walked among his animals, petting them. The camels lifted their dripping muzzles to him, and nuzzled their heads against his hands.

He quietly took out a gold nose-ring, a half-coin in weight, and two carved bracelets. Rebecca looked down at them, nestled in his broad hands. They gleamed warmly; burnished metal against his weathered skin. Then he reached for her arms, one after the other, and put the bracelets on. They felt warm against her skin, the lustrous metal glowing like the sun. He moved toward her to put the nose-ring on, too, but Rebecca stepped back and put out her hand for it.

She held it in her palm. Then she slipped it on her nose herself. It seemed inevitable, this action, this jewelry, his broad hands, and her steady fingers. The well beside her whispered the faintest hollow splash of water.

He said, "Whose daughter are you? Pray, tell me," in a soft voice. He asked, "Is there, perhaps in your father's house, a place for us to spend the night?"

She said, "I am the daughter of Betuel, whose mother is Milca and whose father is Nahor. Yes, there is straw, yes, plenty of fodder for the camels to eat, and yes, there is a place to spend the night."

The man nodded his head in a dignified way each time she said yes, and then bowed low before empty air and said, "Blessed be

the Lord, God of my master, Abraham, who has not relinquished his faithfulness and his trustworthiness from my master!

"While as for me, God has led me on the journey to the house of my master's brothers!"

Rebecca ran and told everyone in her household what had happened. Her brother, Laban, came and listened. He noticed the bracelets on her arms, and the nose-ring she had been given.

He came closer, running his finger along the carving in one of the bracelets. He slipped it off her arm without a word to her, weighed it in his hand, bit it, threw it back at her and turned suddenly and ran off toward the spring. Rebecca picked up the gold bracelet from the dust near her feet.

Rebecca walked to the hill overlooking the spring as the sun sank, sending out one last, coppery sheen of light. Two men and ten camels were outlined in gold over the dark water. She stood still, watching from a distance. Her brother was bowing low as she approached.

"Come, you who are blessed by God! Do not stand outside."

The man followed her brother back, his camels walking slowly behind him. He came onto their land and unbridled his camels. He made sure there was straw and fodder for the animals. He was invited into the house, and offered a chair to sit on. Laban came with a basin and a cloth and washed his feet. He was given food. The man sat before the food and said he could not eat until he had spoken.

Laban sat down, urging the man to speak even before his father, Betuel, came. The man would not speak, though. He waited in silence while Laban beckoned to the women of the household and gave orders for additional foods that were to be served. Women hid behind the cloths at the doors and windows and watched as Betuel entered and sat down next to his son.

The man said, "I am Abraham's servant, Eliezer. I came to wait by the well to see who would be gracious to me. Even before I had finished speaking in my heart, Rebecca came out, her pitcher on her shoulder. She went down to the spring and drew water. I said to her: 'Pray, give me to drink!'

"She was most gracious, and in homage I bowed low, and blessed the God of my master, Abraham, who led me on a journey to find a wife for his son."

Laban and Betuel shrugged, saying, "The matter has come from God, we cannot speak anything to you, evil or good. Here is

Rebecca before you, take her and go, that she may be a wife for the son of your master, as God has spoken."

Laila had come to Rebecca, and standing next to her, she listened to the words, straining to hear through the doorway. She held Rebecca's hand. The stars came out in the darkening sky, lighting up the tears in her eyes. For once she could not speak or joke. She hugged Rebecca and stepped away quietly into the night.

"I will come in the morning."

Before bedding down, Eliezer offered gifts to Rebecca's mother and brother. He gave many gifts to Rebecca, too.

In the morning the noises of the household were louder than they had ever been. The second wife of Betuel hit a wife of Laban. Rebecca's mother had a long argument with the first wife of Laban over a cooking pot. The sound of nasal singing was heard, and then abruptly ceased.

Betuel and Laban were heard arguing, but emerged to act surprised that Eliezer actually wanted to start back as soon as possible. They stood with Rebecca's mother and called Rebecca, very annoyed, and told her they wanted her opinion as to whether she should go as soon as she could make ready, or whether she would stay with her family longer, perhaps ten days or ten months.

Rebecca said, "I will go."

"You will go?" They turned to each other.

"Well, and should we have to send anyone to accompany her?"

"Who could be spared?"

"Will we be compensated for the loss of the labor of a good worker?"

"Maybe she can go alone, she is a strong girl."

Deborah, the mute old nurse, got up and walked to stand next to Rebecca. The family stopped talking, and Rebecca looked at them standing quietly for the first time, and sighed. Then Betuel told his wives to get back to work and these wives ordered Laban's wives back to the cookfire and the two men turned to Eliezer for more discussion of the terms of engagement and it wasn't until later that all was made ready for a leave-taking.

Laila came and gave Rebecca her own tiny god statue, but Rebecca handed it back to her, saying she wanted to learn more about the one God. She gave her friend a beaded bracelet, and Laila gave her a bracelet she had woven herself from goat's hair. Rebecca put this on, and never took it off.

The friends knew that they would never see each other again. They kissed and hugged and wished each other well, giving a blessing of gentle husbands and sweet children and a safe journey through life.

Rebecca's family gave her a blessing of farewell and said, "Our sister, may you become the mother of thousands! May your children inherit the gates of those who hate them!"

Rebecca looked for Laila one last time, and the two of them laughed across the compound into each other's eyes. Rebecca imagined Laila's voice in her ear. "Mother of thousands! Who will change all those diapers!" And she would say "Inherit the gate? Why not the house? What would we do with a gate in our hands?"

The journey was long and hard. Rebecca came to trust Eliezer, and she asked him many questions about his camels and he answered, telling her they were gentle if you treated them gently, and they all had personalities that she could learn about. She asked many questions about her bridegroom, too, but Eliezer would answer none of them. When she saw her husband, Isaac, for the first time, she was surprised that he was so old. She looked toward Eliezer, but he was not Laila, and he did not meet her eye.

Rebecca was suddenly frightened. Will he be cruel? Would her new home be even worse than the old one? Eliezer would not look up at her.

Slowly she turned to Isaac. He was gazing steadily at her, taking her in. He did not say a word to her, but put out his hand. She took his hand. It was warm and firm and welcoming.

A gentle husband, yes, and a quiet one perhaps. Rebecca smiled, turning the goat hair bracelet on her wrist.

6

Rebecca Talks with God

Rebecca was pregnant, resting her hand lightly on a stomach at war with itself. It seemed to her that the whole quarreling mass of her relatives from Aram Naharayim were in her stomach, punching at each other, hitting each other with cook pots, and creeping close in the night to pound new tent posts into her flesh. After twenty years of marriage to her peaceful husband, she wasn't used to such turmoil anymore. The pain was astounding as her stomach hurt, first on one side, and then the other. She didn't know what to do with herself. She kept wondering why this was happening to her. Why did she even exist if this had to be happening to her? What was she to do with a life that seemed turned inside out?

Rebecca went out to watch the camels in their corral. Armisael came slowly toward her, chewing her cud. Rebecca reached out to pet the beast's silly-looking head, letting her fingers slide over the soft face. Armisael blinked her eyes with the long lashes and

solemnly rubbed her head against Rebecca's hand. Rebecca leaned her head next to the camel's cheek.

"Who saddled you?" she whispered to the animal. "That's the saddle I use."

Armisael responded by lowering herself to the ground.

"Stop!" Rebecca was laughing. "I didn't tell you to kneel, you silly camel." She often thought Laila had sent her Armisael. She whispered to the animal sometimes, telling her the funny things Laila would have laughed at.

With Armisael's head so close to her own, Rebecca stroked the long neck and whispered to the camel that her stomach seemed to be developing a whole household of screaming wives, throwing their knives and cleavers at each other. Armisael closed her eyes slowly, nodded her head like she understood, and Rebecca laughed like she used to with her friend.

"You understand," she said, "Isaac is too happy to sympathize. He thinks every bit of this is a blessing, sweet man, even the discomfort is a direct gift from God." She petted Armisael's nodding head. "He brings me water from the Jordan to drink; it should ease the discomfort. Water? My stomach throws each sip from one side to another like a stone. What am I going to do?"

Armisael nudged her toward the saddle and Rebecca smiled. "How could I . . . ?" but she found herself climbing up onto the wide saddle and wedging herself in. Armisael stood up and walked right out of the corral, and Rebecca thought of Laila again. Where was this crazy camel going?

Armisael climbed carefully up the ridge and slowly made her

way along the familiar path away from their tents. It was hot, and Rebecca let her veil fall in front of her face. Maybe no one would see her taking this ride if she kept her face veiled.

She thought maybe she should veil Armisael too, and smiled at the idea of a veiled woman on a veiled camel. She fell asleep for a while, lulled by the rocking gait. Finally, Armisael kneeled again. Gentle hands helped her off the camel, and she was escorted by a servant to a cool cave. She lifted her veil to see an ancient woman smiling at her. The woman gestured, and a man came forward and washed Rebecca's feet. Rebecca pulled away, but the woman insisted.

"My camel is thirsty," Rebecca whispered, but the servant was already returning with an empty bucket. The old woman bade Rebecca to go with her into the cave.

Rebecca followed into the cool depths, walking barefoot on smooth rock, and the old woman's hand seemed to be stronger and stronger as they walked. Finally, the old woman pulled Rebecca back against the cool cave wall. They sat on a bench covered with woven cloth.

Rebecca could feel it when God entered the cave and she stood up to show respect, leaning against the old woman's shoulder. Standing, she listened with all her might. There was a trickle of water somewhere, and a hollow sound, as though wind was blowing far away. At first she thought the old woman was talking with her, but this Voice made her shake with awe. The darkness seemed bright with the music of the Voice. The secrets of Rebecca's heart bubbled to the surface and she cried out how it hurt her that the fighting inside her was like the fighting she had left.

She had lived with Isaac for twenty years, opening her hand to every stranger, creating such love around her that her tent glowed with holy light. From her peaceful tent, she didn't understand how such discord could issue forth.

In the darkness she couldn't say why she suddenly felt comforted, as though a mother far more compassionate than her own was rocking her in her arms. She listened as the Voice told her that it took someone who so loved harmony to do what she would need to do. She was to have two sons. The Voice said:

"Two nations are in your womb,
Two separate peoples shall issue from your body;
One people shall be mightier than the other,
And the older shall serve the younger."

Rebecca listened and nodded and turned to leave. She didn't need the old woman to lead her anymore. She made her way through the darkness and out to the chamber where she had sat. She walked to Armisael, and touched her neck and eased down into the saddle.

She knew the way home, each turn, each landmark, each tree by the road. She saw the tents of her people from a distance, the dark woven cloth of her own dwelling glowing with the light of love and accord she had been nurturing for years now. In this glow she would tend her family, and in this glow she would take the actions needed in the days ahead. In this glow, she would remember the Voice and do good.

She knew that the coming years would be full of challenge for her, and that sometimes she would face situations as difficult as the ones she had fled so many years ago. But she was the one who could handle it, and she would know what to do when the time came. As sure as Laila had gifted her with companionship, this new conversation gifted her with faith to see the way things should be. She could feel it, like a whisper in her ear. The future loomed large and discordant in the darkness. She would meet it with her love of harmony, and prevail.

Leah and Rachel

Rachel and Leah were sisters, and opposites. Leah had a lovely singing voice, and she could cook and bake and weave. Rachel, who ran wildly over the hills as a shepherdess, was so beautiful that everyone who saw her loved her. Rachel was joyful in her life, and Leah often raised the red eyes of jealousy.

It was so hot in the afternoon that all the sheep were brought to the well to drink. The sheep were bleating for water and the shepherds called to each other as they got ready to push the heavy boulder off the well.

Leah came out of her tent as the flocks of sheep were brought in for watering. She sang as she walked toward the well with her pitcher balanced on her head. Across the field her sister, Rachel, walked with her father's flock, repeating Leah's song in a quiet voice.

By the time they reached the well, Leah could feel sweat rolling

down her face. The shepherds were having trouble, yelling at each other as they tried to make the large rock move. Leah watched for a few moments, then beckoned to Rachel to follow her onto the little hill by the well. Rachel stood on the crest of the hill so she could see her sheep.

Leah looked up at the sun and started singing a song she had composed, letting her voice ring out. Rachel joined in with her, her quieter voice half swallowed by the bleating.

From where they stood, Leah could see a stranger approaching. He was tired, almost stumbling.

Leah saw him walking toward the shepherds, a young man with a beard who looked like he had come a long, dusty way. Everything about him was dirty and tired and disheveled. But when he looked up he had light eyes and, to Leah, the face of an angel.

He had heard her singing above the noise of the sheep, but when he looked up he saw only Rachel, standing sentinel at the top of the hill. He smiled at Rachel, impressed. "You sing beautifully," he called up, and Rachel thanked him because she didn't, but it was kind of him to say so.

He heard my voice and he praised her for it, thought Leah. *She should tell him.*

The stranger turned to the shepherds, who had taken a break from their pushing, and leaned into the rock that they had been trying to move. Perhaps he had a surge of strength, as he was falling in love with Rachel, while Leah stood, falling in love with him. The rock sprang off the well and the story of Jacob loving Rachel and Leah loving Jacob and Rachel not loving anyone as yet, began.

Rachel ran down the hill to bring in her flocks. The shepherds told Jacob who she was, and Jacob kissed Rachel when he learned she was a member of his family. When Leah came down off the hill he was already crying tears of joy, and embraced her clumsily before turning back to behold the luminous Rachel.

Laban seemed glad to receive Jacob into the household. He was family, Laban said, and he was curious to hear Jacob's story about fleeing his twin brother, Esau. Jacob said that he had the blessing of his father and continued the family's worship of the one invisible God.

Laban loved hearing the story of Jacob pushing the rock. "You are strong," he said approvingly. Then he invited Jacob to live with them. Jacob brought no idols, but he showed them how he prayed to his one God and was often seen in quiet prayer.

At the town well, a woman named Laila told Leah stories about Jacob's mother, Rebecca. They had been good friends, she said, caressing a beaded bracelet on her wrist. She said Rebecca had hated her family's constant arguing. She had refused the little idol Laila tried to give her, because she loved the idea of the one God. Laila laughed. "That was my dear friend, Rebecca, for you. She knew one God wouldn't be quarreling with itself. One God ruling quietly over everything, telling people to be good to each other; that would be Rebecca's choice."

Laban watched Jacob with Rachel, rushing to help her in all she did. He sent Jacob and Rachel out as shepherds together.

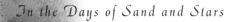

Leah's delicate eyes were getting redder by the day. Laban let the situation ripen for a month and then offered to pay Jacob for his help. He looked surprised when Jacob proposed working seven years for Rachel.

Laban moved Rachel's flocks away from Jacob's. He made sure Jacob's flocks were closer to the household. He encouraged Leah's delectable cooking and told Leah to sing her beautiful songs when Jacob was near.

"Why, Father, when you have already promised him Rachel?" Leah asked.

Laban bit his lip in anger, and Leah stepped back.

"It is enough that I ask," her father said. "Do as I tell you."

The day of Rachel's wedding to Jacob came. Rachel was dressed and decorated and paraded around the compound. Jacob watched her progress from his own tent, his eyes glowing with pleasure.

Leah wept as she dressed. She came out of the tent she shared with Rachel and found her father waiting.

Laban said to her, "Why such red eyes for a bride?"

"I am not a bride, Father."

"But you are. This is your wedding day. I have brought beautifully woven cloth for your veil."

Leah was mystified. She stood and stared.

Laban said, "What! My daughter is acting like a wild heifer today! Come here, come to me and let me arrange this veil. It is your wedding day. Yes, you."

Leah slowly did as her father told her.

Laban hugged her, "Keep yourself veiled."

Leah veiled herself and followed her father. She could hardly see through the thick cloth he had given her to put over her head.

Leah could hear the singing and flute playing as she stood, blind to what was around her. She realized with horror that she was standing next to Jacob under the marriage canopy. She swallowed hard. She was actually being married to Jacob, who wouldn't be able to see in through the cloth anymore than she could see out. He would still think he was marrying Rachel.

Under the heavy woolen veil, she felt she was alone for the first time in her life. She could hardly hear what was being said, and she could see nothing but the tops of her sandals. Sweat coursed down her body in the heat of the afternoon.

Leah thought of the fights that were ahead of her when Jacob realized he was cheated out of his chosen bride and Rachel found out she was cheated out of her wedding day. She remembered Laila, suddenly, talking at the town well about how Rebecca had hated quarrels, and loved the idea of one God. Here, alone under her veil, she was convinced that she was standing in front of this God. She remembered the words that Jacob often said. *Blessed are You, Oh God…* and she said them, and continued, in the most peaceful moment of her life. "May I serve you in peace. May my life be fulfilled in a full household with many children living under Your care." In her mind she heard assent, in her mind she felt surrounded by love, in her mind she prepared herself for her life when the veil was lifted, and a Leah with dry eyes and a sure gaze would step forth.

Rachel and Leah

Leah never reminded her that she had so many more children, but then, she didn't have to. Rachel could count. As a shepherdess she counted sheep all day long. As a mother she counted to one, over and over. One son. Joseph.

At night, Leah's beautiful lullabies filled the air. Many people drifted close to Leah's tent to hear her singing her children to sleep. Long after the children were breathing deeply, Leah's intricate rhythms filled the air and wove themselves into everyone's thought. Rachel listened, her heart aching. Leah sang:

"Each of you has gifts to bear . . .
Raise your voice without a care
Each of you is strong and bold
You'll conquer and win and have and hold . . ."

Rachel's head pounded. How were little Joseph's gifts going to be noticed among so many older brothers? Was he destined to go through life as a servant to them? He was younger, and he took after her, so small and delicate that he would never stand tall among his older brothers. He insisted on following them around the tents, trying to do whatever they did.

Rachel imagined a giant set of brass scales looming above her, casting a dark shadow in the night air. Even if she climbed into the pan on one side with little Joseph, her sister's six sons would still outweigh them both, making her life as light as her voice, always drowned out by her sister.

Rachel took Joseph out to the flocks, where she felt most at home, taking her place among the shepherds as she always had. It was here that she felt peaceful, counting and recounting the gentle sheep in her care. It was good to get away from Leah's beautiful voice and Leah's rambunctious boys. She showed Joseph how to send her dogs out to move the herds, whistling and pointing in the direction she wanted to move. Her little son followed her, his dark eyes bright with dreaming.

Jacob came into Rachel's tent in the evening, and he watched her moving about in the dim light. Joseph sat in his father's lap. Jacob stroked his young son's hair, letting his hand linger on the dark curls. "The littlest boys grow up to be powerful men," he said. Rachel smiled. She knew that Jacob, also, had a much larger older brother. "They need to use their brains, little Joseph. Then all the games don't matter at all." Joseph leaned back into his father's arms.

Leah's lilting voice came through the open entryway. Jacob smiled. Rachel turned away to adjust the tent flap.

Rachel took her son out to the sheep every day, teaching him all she knew about the shepherding traditions of her people. He learned to take responsibility for all the helpless lives resting in their care, finding water, finding good forage, moving them gently, without scaring them. She taught him to learn about the sheep and goats, to know their needs and their fears, and treat them well. There were ways to make them feel secure and content, ways to help the flocks increase and flourish. Rachel was respected among the shepherds as the finest shepherd. This was why, despite her status as a wife in the family, she still went out. Even Laban knew his wealth grew best with Rachel tending some of the flocks.

Out in the fields, under the vast blue skies, Jacob would come to visit Rachel, as he had since his arrival. As overseer, he made sure all the shepherds were managing their flocks well, but he spent extra time with Rachel. They watched little Joseph moving confidently among the sheep, petting the lambs, giving choice grasses to the big ewes. It was here that Jacob told Rachel he wanted to go back to the land of his birth.

"My father will send you away with nothing," she said.

"No. I will think of a way to be paid for all I have done."

"Think carefully. He is a master trickster," Rachel said. She raised her voice to call Joseph to them. "Look, your father is here, my son." The child came running to them.

"Do you want to come home with me and see where I was

born?" Jacob asked his son. "You could see the land of Canaan, our land that we were given by God."

Joseph nodded happily, pressing into his father's legs until Jacob easily picked him up and held him.

Rachel said. "My father might think it a nice joke to send you back with nothing but the clothes you came with. He would want to keep his grandchildren for the future, his daughters to serve him, and all the flocks for his wealth."

Little Joseph closed his eyes on Jacob's chest. "You know everything about the sheep, mother. Tell Father your stories."

Rachel laughed, her eyes focused on the sheep, even as she was talking to them. "I know your mother's stories," Jacob said. "She has told me how to treat the sheep gently, and how to train the dogs not to scare them."

Rachel smiled, "I have been telling Joseph how to breed for different types of wool."

"She taught me that she can change their colors," Joseph said. "I want to see a red and yellow sheep."

Rachel was watching the lambs play at the far northern edge of the flock. She didn't like the lambs so close to the edges. There were lions around who would pounce in a minute on such a quick kill. She whistled and pointed, and her favorite dog, Raafi, wheeled and ran toward the little ones.

"Not colors," she said, distracted, "I said there is an old folk tale that says the sheep will reproduce dark or light, spotted or speckled, according to what they see when they breed."

Jacob straightened up, almost dropping Joseph. "What?"

Rachel waved to Raafi that he had done a good job. She turned to see Jacob staring at her. "The old shepherds used to say that there are so few dark sheep and so few light goats. There are almost no speckled animals that occur naturally. But if you were to have the animals reproduce where they could see dark and light objects they might have dark and light offspring. Speckled. Spotted."

"I would make you a coat, Mother, that looks like the sunrise."

Rachel laughed, her eyes scanning the flocks again. "When I first told that story to Joseph he said he would make me a coat with all the colors that the sheep saw. . . ."

"Green for grass," the little boy said. "White for clouds. Blue for the sky."

Jacob wasn't laughing. "Does it work?"

Something in his voice made Rachel turn away from the flocks again. "When we were little, some of the kids once tried setting up a shaded area for the sheep to mate in. We set it up by the troughs. There were actually a few dark sheep born that year." She laughed, looking up at her husband. "We were not too consistent though. Some days we ran away and went dipping in the spring instead."

That night Jacob dreamed about dark sheep and spotted and speckled goats.

When Jacob went to talk with Laban he took Joseph with him.

"My littlest son had an idea for my wages," Jacob said. "We will take only the dark sheep and the spotted and speckled goats. He likes rare animals. He wants to make his mother a very unusual coat."

Laban agreed right away, his smile as wide as his embracing arms.

"Of course, my son. You are welcome to take those animals."

Laban immediately culled the few speckled and spotted goats and the dark sheep. He then directed that the remaining sheep and goats be taken a three-day journey away, so the two flocks could not mix. He sent his sons to watch these flocks.

Leah sang alone in her tent, as her sons went with Laban's sheep and goats. The sons of the serving maids, Bilhah and Zilpah, went too, and they followed all that Jacob said to do regarding the mating of the animals.

Jacob worked in the fields with his older sons, setting up special rods for the goats to mate under. He had the boys take fresh shoots of poplar and almond, and plane trees and peel white stripes in them, laying bare the white of the shoots. He set up the light and dark rods in front of the goats at the long water troughs. The animals mated when they came to drink, and, true to Rachel's story, when the goats gave birth, the little kids were streaked and speckled and spotted.

Jacob ordered that the animals in all the flocks should mate while watching streaked or dark objects. Soon there were many more streaked or dark lambs to put with his animals. He discussed his plans with Rachel beforehand, and she reminded him that he would probably want very sturdy animals to bring along with them. Jacob agreed with her, and made sure he only bred the strongest sheep and goats in this unusual way. Soon, his herds became numerous and strong. The flocks that Laban had thought would be small and insignificant, became substantial. Jacob's family grew exceedingly prosperous, and came to own large flocks, maidservants and menservants, camels and donkeys.

Rachel, in the first months of her second pregnancy, could not go out for the three-day journey to the flocks. She stayed in the camp with Joseph, listening to him prattle about the coat he would make her, while Leah's songs swirled around them. The enforced resting period, coupled with Joseph's restlessness and the relentless beauty of Leah's songs, seemed to Rachel promise that nothing would come easy in this family. Perhaps, as Jacob sometimes said, their family would receive blessings from God. Rachel listened and worried. It wouldn't come easily, she knew that. In this family, events would always be throwing their long shadows across people, and the future would be striped and speckled and sometimes dark beneath them.

Dina, Weaver of Invisible Dreams

In their home in the desert, the sands were tan and the sky was pale and the sun seared everything in sight brown and dead. Dina stayed in her tent for a whole summer, trying to forget that she had met a young man from Shechem when she went walking. He had seized her and taken her into his house and kept her there, until her brothers came to rescue her. While her mother, Leah, held her too tight, her older brothers carried out their revenge. The thumping of their camels' feet marked their departure and their return. They tried to talk to her, but she turned away. She didn't even want to understand.

Now she was afraid to leave her tent. She let minutes lengthen into hours, and hours lengthen into days without moving. She had not left her tent or spoken of what happened to her, not to anyone.

Her half brother, Joseph, came into the tent quietly and sat with her. Raafi came with him, wagging his tail in greeting, watching over them both with calm shepherding eyes. It came easily to Joseph, still mourning his mother's death, to sit with her, as quiet as the sands, comforting her with nothing more than his presence.

Joseph's green eyes reminded her of the summer when they had gone swimming in the sheep's watering hole. Their playful movements had stirred up the silt at the bottom of the hole, and the shepherds had hauled them out disgustedly, threatening to tell their father, Jacob. Joseph had been laughing, but that stopped him pretty quickly.

"Don't tell," Dina pleaded quickly. "We won't do it again."

The shepherds held tight to Joseph and Dina and argued about what to do until Rachel's flocks arrived for their turn at the well.

The shepherds turned to Rachel. Dina could feel the calm touch of her beautiful aunt's gaze, hovering over her like a protective cloak.

"It will be dark before the sheep can drink here now," the shepherds said disgustedly. "We have to teach these children a lesson."

Rachel nodded in agreement. "They will stay with the sheep while all the shepherds withdraw to rest. They will have to work hard for the time of waiting, keeping the thirsty sheep calm. Then, they will haul water for the flocks."

Dina and Joseph had stayed with the sheep while Rachel sat down under a nearby tree. She was pregnant, but she stayed awake in the intense heat, and let them use her well-trained dogs to control the flocks.

This memory evaporated as Dina shifted, and Joseph looked up. It was over a year later, and Rachel had died during their journey to this new home in Canaan. Her soft voice was replaced with baby Benjamin's wail. Rachel's dogs had been taken over by the other shepherds, except for Raafi, who followed Joseph like he was the last sheep left in the world.

Leah was so busy raising Benjamin that she had little time for Dina, and Joseph was so protected by his father that no one even suggested the boy leave his home tents to tend the herds. That left the two of them sitting, day after day near Leah's loom, filling the space between them with nothing. The taste of nothing was in their mouths, and the faraway smells and sounds of a happier life grew dimmer by the moment.

Jacob came into the tent one day, looking for Leah, and found his two children, sitting idle. He frowned, but said nothing. The next day, he sent Joseph on an errand. While Joseph was gone, he entered the tent.

"Joseph is having a hard time getting over the death of his mother," he said. "I want you to help me give him something that will remind him that he has to live."

Dina, accustomed to listening closely to all her father wanted, leaned forward.

"I have brought you special wool from our speckled and spotted sheep," he said. "They have produced fine rich wool with mingled shadings of color. You will make Joseph a coat that will remind him of all he could be. I will give you beautiful gold thread from the Egyptian traders to edge it with. It will be a coat fit for royalty, and he will wear it proudly."

Leah's loom lay still behind her. Dina took the wool in her hands and smoothed it down. It was as soft and smooth as Rachel's voice had been and it seemed to whisper a promise to her. Dina said, "The wool needs to be spun into thread…"

"Yes, of course," her father said, "and you will do it. I will not let Joseph sit without purpose. He will remember himself when he sees this coat."

Dina smelled the wool, remembering the ragged bleating of the sheep on that long day when they waited to drink. The sheep had milled around, puzzled at the empty troughs. She and Joseph had pretended to be Rachel, whistling the dogs around, pulling the lambs and kids to safety within the large flock.

"The coat should be unique and beautiful," Jacob said. "It will remind Joseph of the coat he dreamed about for my Rachel."

Dina looked up to her father. His voice had shaken when he said his favorite wife's name. Dina wondered what it would feel like to be so loved.

Dina carded the heavy wool with Joseph, picking out burrs and twigs. Joseph helped, never asking what she was doing. She spun the wool out. Leah came in carrying little Benjamin, who seemed to be trying to make up for delicate Joseph in the volume of his bawling. Dina watched her half brother and thought that she was more like Joseph than this yowling being would ever be. His screaming split the silence of the tent. They began to talk more, as Joseph held up his hands square and steady, one cubit apart, and she wound the yarn around them into skeins, which she hung from the ceiling.

Joseph told her that he missed his mother's quiet eyes, eyes that could measure up a flock's movements in a minute. "She thought I could do great good," he said. "That was her assessment. You know how she would predict what the sheep were going to do. She predicted me and was so happy…." He shrugged. "Now that is all gone."

Dina stopped winding yarn. "At first I thought the man who took me looked at me like our father looked at your mother; with such adoration. It made me think she was back. Then he tore at me like an animal." Tears came at last. Dina cried into the yarn she held.

"God will bless the work of your hands," Joseph said suddenly, in a quiet, sure voice so like Rachel's, that they looked at each other in shock, and then both started laughing.

Dina waved the wool in her hands, laughing in great gusts. "This very work – from dotty sheep…."

A cool wind blew through the raised tent flaps, bringing the smell of dillweed.

Leah helped Dina string up the loom. She hummed while she worked, and Benjamin stopped trying to tangle up the yarn, and they all listened to the music of Leah's baby songs.

When the yarn went into the loom the streaked and speckled and spotted tones seemed to resolve themselves into intricate patterns. Dina was amazed at the cloth that issued forth as she

threw the shuttle across. When Jacob came to look, he smiled at her.

"This is what I wanted. You are doing a good job."

Leah helped Dina cut and stitch the cloth to form it into a coat. Jacob brought the gold trim he had obtained from Egyptian traders. Joseph was sent to chase Benjamin around the camp, involving him in a wild game with Raafi, who was happy to dodge back and forth, herding again.

One night Jacob asked that a special meal be prepared for the next dinner. The whole camp smelled like lamb and dill and cumin and mint as it was cooked the following day. Shortly after sundown when the sheep had been watered, the ten sons filed in, one by one, jostling each other until their father called for the meal to begin. Flat pita breads were passed from hand to hand around the table. The delicate spices Leah had used enhanced the smells and tastes, making them remarkable and piquant, just like Leah's voice had always turned bedtime songs into glorious music.

After a delicious dinner Jacob stood up, and the family stilled. Even Benjamin looked up. Jacob beckoned to Dina, and when she came to him, he sent her out of the tent. All were quiet – even the sheep – and the whirring of the crickets and the croak of toads outside dropped away. When she came back, Dina carried something folded. The long, muted hoot of an owl lingered in the air and then faded.

Jacob nodded his thanks and Dina went back to her seat. Jacob held the coat up. He beckoned to Joseph, who came to his father slowly. Jacob put the garment around Joseph's shoulders, and Joseph slipped his arms through the sleeves.

There was not a sound in the room as Joseph turned around, marveling at the creation he wore.

From her seat next to her mother, Dina could see how some of the patterns in the cloth looked like lines of writing from one of the ancient scrolls her father studied. Now that she stood apart from the garment, she was amazed at what it had become. The fire burning behind Joseph made the dark hues dance across the ivory background. Joseph pulled the coat around him, smiling. His shadow stretched across the table, suddenly huge in the dancing flames.

To Dina it seemed like everybody was holding their breath, until a slow beating was heard as Raafi began wagging his tail against the floor. Then Joseph called her to him and hugged her, and they stood together with the coat that she had made out of her father Jacob's idea and her mother Leah's loom and the wool from beautiful Aunt Rachel's sheep and her own sure touch.

Two weeks later, Dina was minding Benjamin for her mother when Joseph came to talk about his dreams. She watched one half brother toddling exuberantly from tent post to tent post, while the other spoke so softly, she could hardly hear him as he recounted his dreams.

"I was a sheaf of wheat. The rest of the family were sheaves too, and they bowed down to me."

Dina jumped up to keep Benjamin from going too close to the fire, but Raafi got there first, skillfully cutting him off before he could burn himself. Benjamin sat down hard on his behind and cried, and Dina turned to Joseph.

"I know some people who are going to be steamed when they hear that one," she warned. Joseph didn't hear her; he continued with his second dream. "All of us were stars and my father, Jacob, was the sun and my mother, Rachel, the moon and they all bowed down to my star."

"Oh, right, that should go down better," Dina said sarcastically. "Even Father and Aunt Rachel . . ."

She felt as though someone had just told her the sheep had taken over and were herding the people. "This isn't right, Joseph, and you are going to be so sorry if you tell. . . ."

Joseph leaned toward her, on fire with his vision. "I know it came from God. It made me fall down to the ground with my eyes open, and I didn't see anything around me, only those dreams. They were trimmed with gold like my coat. . . ."

Dina sat back and watched him. Raafi was licking Benjamin, and the little boy was trying to grab his wagging tail. Dina kept her eye on them while she talked with Joseph.

"Then I suppose this isn't the time to tell you that the coat is making the brothers angry . . ."

"The feeling was exhilarating," he said. "I wish you could feel it, Dina. It made me so happy, like I was eating a cloud filled with light."

"NO!" Dina said. They all turned to look at her, dog and boys, while she leaned forward to Joseph. "Can't you hear what I'm saying to you?"

Benjamin was still, so she risked taking her eyes off him to focus on Joseph. She glared at him, letting the question hang in the air like a drop of rain that will not fall, hovering in front of his face. Joseph blinked, and for a moment Rachel's lovely eyes seemed to look out at her. When Rachel looked at you, there was always a connection.

"Joseph, you have to come back to earth," she said. Even as she spoke, she could tell that Joseph was not listening. "Some things are not for sharing," she said. "People will not understand."

Joseph nodded slowly.

"Promise me you won't tell our brothers," Dina said. "Promise me you will stay home when they go out with the sheep."

"It is time for me to work," he said. "I can't mourn my mother forever."

Dina put her hand on her favorite brother's arm. Beneath her hand the coat she had woven for him was spelling out a message she couldn't read. The black designs were almost letters, and there might almost be advice in them.

In the morning, the older brothers prepared to go out to the far fields with the sheep. Dina had been given Benjamin to tend while her mother prepared food for them. Joseph stood apart, observing his brothers, the coat pulled around him like a sheep's growing fleece, fine and strong and substantial.

As the flocks were moved out, the dogs ran around the edges, barking to keep the sheep in line. The hot sun bathed them all in strange light. The brothers took their leave of their parents, their eyes flickering over Dina.

Was it her imagination that they looked strangely at Joseph, the brother who was different? Dina watched Raafi for a minute and then yelled to Levi to whistle for him. Raafi's ears perked up and he answered the whistle, leaping toward some silly sheep that were heading in the wrong direction.

None of us can protect him enough, she thought of Joseph. *He will go beyond the sheep and beyond those who want to take care of him. His way will be hard and we cannot smooth it.* She felt strange and light-headed, as though the thoughts were flowing into her from above, just like her brother had said.

Raafi can't help him and I can't help him and even his coat will fall away. I know this.

She felt like Rachel making one of her predictions about the flock's direction. *I will have to go on without Joseph.* He was still there, standing alone in his gorgeous coat with his hand raised in farewell.

Soon, he will leave. And I will go on.

The brothers left with the flocks. The sound of the bleating became softer. Raafi's plumy tail disappeared into the distance. Joseph's eyes were fixed on the sky. Already, he was far away. Already. She put out her hand to Benjamin and took him in to lunch.

Yocheved, God's Glory

Yocheved was raised on the old stories. Her nurse, old Sarah Dina, never tired of telling her that she herself was named after two women. "One with red hair like a rooster's comb and a crow of laughter. That was the Sarah part, my sweetest Yocheved. The name Dina came from the great weaver, who created the coat that has been passed down among our people as a sign of hope."

Yocheved said she wanted to see this coat, but Sarah Dina couldn't be stopped when she got on the subject of names. "And your own name means *God's glory*. And what do you think you will do to earn this glory, little one?"

In time, her children, Aaron, Miriam, and Moses would be her glory and God's, too. But for now, Yocheved didn't know. She was six. She had been taught that God is as strong as her father and as gentle as her mother, but she didn't have the slightest idea what

she could do to become God's glory. Her parents worked all day and into the night building storage cities for the Egyptians. When she asked Sarah Dina if that was the glory – the completed cities – Sarah Dina looked away.

"That would make you Pharoah's glory, not God's. It is not to be achieved by hauling bricks."

Yocheved was less interested in predicting her life achievements than in seeing Joseph's woven coat. She begged to see the coat every day, patiently moving them one step closer with every request. One day, Sarah Dina finally took her by the hand into sun so hot it could blister you with a single bright glance. They walked to the hut of an elderly man named Manesseh, and Yocheved was made to repeat back his geneology. He was named after the eldest son of the great Joseph, who had saved us all from starvation. Who had brought us to Egypt, a proud people with a beautiful history.

Yocheved hid behind Sarah Dina as the bent old man with the white hair shuffled into the back room to show them an old trunk. It took the combined strength of the two old people to raise the lid, but then Yocheved stepped forward to look inside at the ancient fragment of garment. At first she thought this must be the rag that wrapped the great coat. It was a curious piece, not like the shining garments of the Egyptian royalty.

She made as if to touch it, and Sarah Dina moved to restrain her.

Manesseh said, "No, let the girl touch it. It is all we have left." Sarah Dina held her wrist for a minute and then let it go. "Go ahead then, little one."

Yocheved reached out again, her hand shaking now, and she smoothed the wool, tracing the intricate design on the fine fabric. A smell like the dill growing in the fields filled the air. She looked up at Manesseh who nodded. "We were a great people once," he said.

Sarah Dina said, "We had our own lands and we raised our cattle and sheep on them as our ancestors did long ago. We were a free people."

Yocheved walked home, her hand safely tucked in Sarah Dina's dry grasp. Sarah Dina made her trace Manesseh's lineage back to Joseph yet again, and recount how Joseph had been a great leader, shepherding his people like his mother, Rachel, had watched over the flocks. A great people, once. A great people, long ago.

As they made their way down the hot dusty roads of Goshen, Sarah Dina dipped back into her stories again, and Yocheved's mind filled with images of past greatness. How Joseph had come to Egypt and helped Pharoah understand his dreams, and how his family had finally come to join him, bringing the coat he had worn as a young man. They had settled in Egypt and prospered in raising sheep and cattle many years ago.

"Were you alive then?" Yocheved asked. "Did you see Joseph?"

"When I was little we could still go to worship in our way," Sarah Dina sniffed. "That was enough."

Yocheved could feel her skin burning to ashes under the hot sun. The walk took even longer coming home. Sarah Dina was going on about how beautiful it had been, all they had lost — all they had lost and how they had only their old stories — until Yocheved was overcome with annoyance.

She stopped in the middle of the road, stunted grain framing them on either side, and stamped her foot. "We haven't lost it all, then, have we? We still have the stories!"

Sarah Dina turned away bitterly, "It's all we have, little Yocheved. You yourself will be pulling up straw for bricks in another year. You will spend your youth working as a slave for Pharoah, and you will have children to be his slaves in the future."

Yocheved could never remember being so angry. Sarah Dina looked so old to her. She seemed like a tiny doll, far away, growing smaller, as she bit her lip to keep from speaking. *It will be different for me,* she thought. *Different.*

When Yocheved was seven she was taken to work, gathering straw. She was forced to work hard every day. In time the whispery voice of Sarah Dina became nothing but a soft memory, a pastel vision fading under the blinding brightness of the desert sun.

By the time Yocheved was thirteen years old, she had worked in the fields for six years. Her hands were scarred and aching from the straw she had to gather every day. One day, the sandy dust in her throat and eyes overwhelmed her. It was hotter than it had ever been, and her mother and father had given her the last of their water and it wasn't enough. She was light-headed and nauseous and then she dropped like an animal, unable to move.

If there had been shade, perhaps her parents would have brought her to it. As it was, her mother adjusted her clothes so she was protected as much as possible, and worked on. The other slaves walked around her. At the end of the day, Yocheved's parents came for her and helped her walk home. She rested while they prepared their meager dinner.

Yocheved lay like a rock in her bed. She smelled the soup her mother was cooking. Her mother must have been trying to make a broth she would really like, because she went out again and brought something new to chop into it. Yocheved smelled the new smell, a delicate green scent. Dill.

Dill. It reminded her of her old nurse, in a life that seemed long ago and infinitely better than the present. She wondered if the old coat she had seen still existed in its trunk, and she began recalling the stories she had been told. There had been a flood, she remembered, and a woman named Naamah had helped her family survive on the Ark. She had talked with the animals and insisted on freedom — with restraints.

The next day Yocheved walked back to work with her family, one hand in each of her parents' hands. They were part of a huge crowd of Hebrew slaves, and as they started working, the dust from their work filled Yocheved's lungs again. She took a heavy load of straw to the people who would mix it with mud and shape it into bricks.

As she let down her load, a handful of straw fell at her feet. She walked back to fetch more straw, carrying it in her hand. The straw tingled in her stiff, raw fingers. Thinking of the story of the Ark, she wove the straw into a little vessel. On her next trip, she was able to get close enough to the brickmakers to get a handful of mud to smooth inside her little boat. She slipped it into her pocket then, and continued with her work.

When she got home, Yocheved took the little straw and mud creation out of her pocket. It was crushed and unrecognizable. Before she went to sleep, she smoothed it out and left it to dry next to her bed. It gave her hope, that little boat. Maybe, someday, she would make a bigger ark. Then her whole people would float away from this misery, back to their land of Canaan, where their laughter would mingle with Sarah's, and their tents would glow with the quiet peace that Rebecca had loved. The people would watch over their sheep, as Rachel had, as their own God watched over them, with the faith that Leah had felt. Their studies would be written – dark patterns against light – and brighten their lives like the designs of the beautiful coat Dina had woven.

Yocheved blinked back tears. *Sarah Dina was wrong,* she thought. *My people will not be slaves forever.*

The sight of the little ark, its sturdy sides and its safe interior, was enough to put her to sleep that night. *Someday, I will just have to make it bigger,* she thought, drifting off. *Some special day, all the old stories will live for us again. We will make our way — back, back, back — to the land where we belong, in the glorious days of countless golden sands beneath our feet and countless sparkling stars to guide us home. Wherever we go we will remember the future promised to us, because we will see it spelled out in what we hold dear: a listening and a laughter from far back in time. We will tell stories forever about the ark, the coat, and the sands, and the stars.*